HOPELEF

CW00867751

CIRCUS
BEASTLY
FEAST

STELLA
TARAKSON

Sweet
Cherry

Published by Sweet Cherry Publishing Limited
Unit 36, Vulcan House,
Vulcan Road,
Leicester, LE5 3EF
United Kingdom

First published in the UK in 2020
2020 edition

2 4 6 8 10 9 7 5 3 1

ISBN: 978-1-78226-351-7

© Stella Tarakson

Hopeless Heroes: Circe's Beastly Feast

Cover design by Nick Roberts and Amy Booth
Illustrations by Nick Roberts

www.sweetcherrypublishing.com

Printed and bound in China
C.WM004

In memory of Tracey Robinson,

an unforgettable friend

Tim Baker couldn't believe it. There must have been a mistake. How could his friends in Ancient Greece have forgotten him? After all they'd been through! It didn't make sense.

Except … maybe it did, Tim thought moodily, staring at his bedroom wall. Maybe Hercules had decided that he couldn't forgive Tim. Not after his daughter got hurt on their last adventure.

Hercules had forbidden him from visiting them once before. The hero had told Tim straight out that he didn't want Zoe to get involved in dangerous adventures. This time was different, though. Hercules didn't seem to know who Tim was. He didn't even recognise the vase, which had been his prison for thousands of years. How could that be? Even Zoe had said she didn't know Tim. And *she* wouldn't pretend. She never held back on her feelings. If she was upset with someone she would say so. Loudly and clearly.

What was going on?

Tim stared at the old Greek vase, at the picture of Hercules wrestling a

bull, at the ancient writing that spoke of the vase's mystery and magic. A lump formed in his throat. Hercules had been trapped in the vase by the queen goddess Hera. By accidentally breaking it, Tim had set the hero free. That was when it had all started – the friendships, the adventures, the chance to do amazing things. And maybe …

… maybe this was where it would all end.

During one of Tim's visits to the past, the messenger god Hermes had repaired the glued-together vase. He'd made it look as good as new, but now Mum wanted to sell it. Because the vase was so old, it was very valuable. Selling it would give her enough money to quit her second job. And then that would be that: no more adventures.

Tim had thought that Hercules and Zoe would worry about him if he never returned, so he'd decided to go back and tell them that the vase was being sold. Only to discover that they didn't know who he was!

Tim wished there was someone he could talk to about his problem. The

8

only person who knew his secret was Mum's boyfriend, Larry. But he had already made it clear that he didn't think Tim should return to Ancient Greece. It was too dangerous. If Tim went to Larry for advice, the teacher would simply sit back, cross his long legs and confirm Tim's deepest fears. His Greek friends thought that he should stay away too. Perhaps this was their way of saying goodbye.

Still, Tim couldn't quite believe it. There *had* to be an explanation for their strange behaviour – but what?

Maybe he could ask the Pythia! Tim grinned as the thought occurred to him. The oracle should be able to help. After all, it was her job to answer people's questions. Tim remembered the time he'd gone to her for advice – that had turned out well in the end. Tim frowned. Last time the Pythia had insisted on a tribute. But what could he give her? Without Zoe's help, he had no idea what a suitable tribute might be. Besides, all the Pythia's

screeching and wailing had given him a headache. Maybe he should go straight to the source of her information – bypass the oracle and ask the god who spoke through her.

APOLLO.

He hadn't been too friendly last time, but that might have been because he'd been preparing for a gig. The god of prophecy was also the god of music – punk music, to be precise. The angry young god was anti-everything and way too interested in vomit. Still, Tim couldn't think of a better idea.

He gripped the magic vase's handles. 'Oh vase, take me to Apollo.'

Tim landed on the steps of a glistening black temple. Clutching the vase to his chest, he crept between the towering columns. Aggressive guitar-like music filled the air and Tim had to shout to be heard over it.

'APOLLO? MR APOLLO, SIR?'

The strumming stopped, and a crotchety voice called from the temple's dark interior. 'Who the Hades is that? Can't you see I'm busy?'

Squinting, Tim saw the slim god sitting cross-legged on the floor. He was holding a lyre.

'Can I talk to you for a minute?' Tim took a step closer.

'Are you deaf? I said I'm busy!' Apollo's mohawk bristled.

'I only–'

'I've written a new song, but I can't think of a rocking title! I'm sick to the Styx of trying! So get lost.'

Tim thought quickly. 'If I can come up with a title for you, will you help me?'

Apollo sniffed. 'Maybe. But it better be good! Here, listen.' The god burst out into a sudden, jerky tune with loud screeching lyrics that made no sense. Tim tried very hard not to clap his hands over his ears. When Apollo

finished, he glared at Tim expectantly. 'Well?'

'Awesome! It'll be a hit,' Tim chirped, hoping the god couldn't read minds. 'How about you call it, err …' He racked his brain for something sufficiently revolting. 'Erm … *Rolling in the Dung Heap?*

'That's a worse idea than *living* in a dung heap! Get out.'

'Okay, okay.' Tim raised his hands in defeat. 'How about *Blame It on the Bogie*? Or, um, *Let It Pee?*

'*Let It Pee.*' Apollo said the words slowly, trying them out. 'Yeah, sick!' Grinning, he scribbled the title on a scrap of parchment. 'Right, you've got ten seconds.'

The words tumbled over each other as Tim hastened to explain his problem.

Apollo curled his pierced lip. 'Sounds simple to me. I reckon you went to the wrong time.'

'W-what do you mean?'

'I mean, phlegm-face, you might have gone back to *before* they'd met you.'

'Hey, yeah! Maybe.'

Tim brightened. It made sense! Normally the vase took him to a time that followed on naturally from the previous one. Maybe something had gone wrong. He had said "take me *back* to Zoe's house." Had it mistakenly taken him too far back? It was possible. Relief washed over him.

'Thanks! I'll try again.'

'Yeah.' Apollo went back to his lyre, muttering. '*Let It Pee …*'

Tim had to make sure that the vase landed at the right time, and not just in the right place. 'Oh vase, take me to Zoe's house,' he said. 'Make sure it's right after her legs were cured by the Golden Fleece gloves.' He thought some more. 'Actually, make it the next morning, a bit after breakfast.' Tim didn't want to turn up too late at night. Besides, his friend needed to recover from her ordeal.

The vase seemed to understand what Tim was saying. It waited until he finished giving his instructions before it lifted him into the air.

Tim landed neatly on Zoe's doorstep. The sun was rising, and the air was cool and fresh. Tim felt hopeful. He put the vase down and knocked on the door. Hercules opened it. By the look of it, the hero was still eating his breakfast. He was chewing, and holding a handful of dark yellow fruits.

'YOU AGAIN!'

Hercules growled. 'Why have you returned? I told you last night – we do not want to buy your amphora.' He glanced scornfully at the vase at Tim's feet.

Tim's stomach lurched. How could this be happening? The vase hadn't taken him to the wrong time after all. 'Why don't you recognise me? We're friends. I know you, and Zoe, and your wife Agatha–'

Hercules' eyes bulged alarmingly. 'Who asked you to come here? What do you want? Are you a thief? A kidnapper?' He glared up and down the street. 'Where is your accomplice?'

'I don't have one!' Tim resisted the urge to clutch at Hercules' chiton. 'I'm not out to hurt you or your family … I'm Tim Baker. From the future. Remember? Hera trapped you in this vase and you were there for thousands of years. I broke it and set you free.'

'What nonsense is this?' Hercules scoffed. 'I have never been trapped in any type of ceramic pot or vessel.' He planted his beefy hands on his hips. 'And how could you say such awful things about

Hera? That wonderful woman is like a mother to me. If you were not a child, I would hurl you into the Underworld for spreading such vicious lies!'

Now Tim knew something was seriously wrong. Hera … wonderful? Like a mother? How could Hercules not remember all the times the wicked goddess had tried to capture them?

'Leave now and don't come back.' Hercules added, 'Next time, I will not be so merciful.' With that, he slammed the door in Tim's face.

Blinking rapidly, Tim picked up his vase and turned away. He had

no idea where to go. Somewhere quiet, where he could sit on his own and think. Why had his friends rejected him and sided with their enemy? It didn't make sense. A tear trickled down his cheek, but he felt too miserable to wipe it away.

Heads turned as Tim walked down the street. He felt out of place in his modern-day outfit of jeans and a T-shirt. Zoe's mother Agatha had made him his very own chiton, but Tim obviously couldn't go and ask for it now. For the first time, he felt as if he didn't belong in Ancient Greece.

'Hello there, little buddy.'

Tim swivelled around at the sound

of the familiar voice. It was Hermes, the messenger god. The wings on his cap and sandals flapped in greeting.

'You know who I am?' Tim asked.

'Course I do!' Hermes tipped his head to the side. 'Shouldn't I,

Tim Baker? Is this some sort of guessing game? Kids from the future have a weird idea of fun.'

'No, it's just …' Tim hesitated. He'd never been too sure about whether he could trust Hermes. There were times when the young god seemed to help Tim, but at other times it was harder to tell. In any case, there was no denying that Hermes was Hera's servant. He was also the god of thieves and liars, which Zoe was always quick to point out.

Zoe. Tim felt a pang of misery, and before he knew it, the words came gushing out. 'It's just that nobody else seems to know who I am.' He put the vase down with a sigh.

'That's odd.' Hermes frowned. He sat on a low wall and gestured for Tim to join him. 'Tell me everything.'

So Tim did. It took a while to get the whole story out, but by the end of it Hermes was nodding. 'Yes, yes, I think I see.'

'What?'

'They're upset that Zoe got injured,' Hermes said, his eyes wide and round. 'Can't blame them, really. Hercules is trying to protect his kid. I think all this forgetting business is just an act.'

This echoed Tim's first thoughts. There was something that still didn't make sense though. 'But then why did he say nice things about Hera?'

'To show how upset he is,' Hermes said promptly. 'He's telling you that she's not the problem – you are.'

'W-WHY?'

'Think about it for a sec. Hercules once banished you because you put Zoe in danger. And now you've only gone and done it again, right?'

Tim felt more tears prickle at his eyes. He nodded.

Hermes placed a firm hand on Tim's shoulder. 'After all, you keep provoking Hera.

Hercules probably thinks that if you stayed away, Zoe would be safe.'

'Gah! I'll have to apologise!' Tim cried. 'I don't want them to hate me.' He slid himself off the wall, but Hermes grasped his shoulder to stop him dashing off.

'I'd leave it for now if I were you,' the god said. 'Give 'em a chance to cool off a bit. Let 'em get over it.'

Tim didn't want to wait. He wanted to sort things out straight away.

'You'll only make it worse,' Hermes warned, not loosening his grip. 'Look, how about this. Let Hercules cool down, and then I'll go talk to him myself. Tell him he's being a jerk and to get over it. But not right now. Can you do that, Tim

Baker? Can you wait, for the sake of your friendship?' The god looked deep into Tim's eyes.

Tim found himself nodding. 'I guess.'

Hermes exhaled. 'Good. Smart kid.' He patted Tim's shoulder.

'So I may as well go home—' Tim started to say.

'Not necessarily.' Hermes slid off the wall and stood next to Tim. 'Actually, I was wondering. Seeing as you're here, could you do me a favour?'

'What sort of favour?' Tim asked. He hoped it didn't involve cleaning again. Tim had enough of that at home.

'I'm behind with my deliveries,' Hermes said.

It took Tim a moment for the meaning to register.

'OH, RIGHT,'

he said. Hermes was the messenger god,

so that must mean it was his job to deliver messages.

'I'm up to my eyeballs,' Hermes said, 'and I've got an urgent parcel. If I don't get it delivered on time, there'll be Hades to pay. I was on my way when I saw you, little buddy. But I had to stop, seeing as how you looked so sad.'

Tim smiled weakly. Then his smile turned into a puzzled frown. He looked around. 'I can't see a parcel ...'

As he spoke, Hermes raised his hand. A stack of huge packages materialised in the air, bobbing above his upturned palm. Some of them were larger than a fridge.

'I can't carry those! They're way too big.'

'Hang on, I think I've got some smaller ones.' Hermes clicked his fingers and the large boxes disappeared, leaving a stack of packages the size of shoe boxes. 'How about one of these? Let me see … the one on top is marked URGENT. How about you grab that one?'

'What's in it?' Tim asked, worried that it might be heavier than it looked.

'How would I know? I'm just the messenger.'

'So can't you – err – magic them to where they need to go? Rather than having to take them there?' Tim thought it was a reasonable question.

'Hah! Don't be silly.' Hermes ruffled Tim's hair. 'It doesn't work like that!'

'Oh.' Tim looked at the small package. 'I don't mind taking it, I guess.'

'GOOD LAD!'

Hermes nodded at the package and it flew into Tim's hands. 'Cheers. I'll get on with my other deliveries, and when we're done we'll go see Hercules and talk some sense into him. Okay?'

Tim brightened. 'Okay!'

'Would you like me to look after your vase for you?' Hermes asked. 'It's too big for you to lug around.' The god reached for the vase, but Tim grabbed it first.

'No, that's all right. I'll hang onto it,' Tim said. It would be a nuisance to take it with him but he wasn't taking any chances. Normally he'd leave it stored safely in Hercules' house, but today that was out of the question.

'You don't trust me?' Hermes asked shrewdly, his eyes fixed on Tim's face.

Tim didn't know what to say to that. He shrugged.

Hermes' wings drooped. 'Can't blame you. Hera's like, my boss, get it? I have to do what she says. But when she's not around' – he winked – 'I can do what I like.'

'I understand,' Tim said. 'But I'll keep it. It's no trouble.'

Hermes sighed. 'Maybe one day, you'll learn to trust me. Then I hope we'll be friends.'

'I hope so too,' Tim said, not making eye contact.

'All righty, that'll have to do.' Hermes watched as Tim hoisted up the vase and struggled to balance it with the parcel. 'Take the package to Narcissus. Do you know where he lives? No? Right, listen up – you don't want to get lost.'

The directions took Tim up a steep hill. It was hard going. The crooked path was little more than a goat track. Sweat poured off his face and his legs began to tremble. He was starting to regret not taking Hermes up on the offer to leave the vase behind. Except … maybe he could use it to travel! It would be much faster and so much easier! Tim tried to shuffle the package and the vase around to get a better grip on the handles, when a loud voice interrupted him.

'FIE!'

Tim swung around. A robust, middle-aged man was sitting by the path in the shade of a tree. Shiny bronze armour glittered on his chest. On his head was a close-fitting leather helmet with large animal teeth sewn all over it. Although his dark hair was flecked with grey, the man had a powerful physique. His tanned arms bulged as he brought a two-handled cup to his lips. He sipped noisily.

'Are you talking to me?' Tim asked, looking left and right.

'I fail to see who else I might be addressing,' the stranger snapped. 'Fie!'

Tim took the opportunity to ease the vase onto the ground. 'Why do you keep saying "fie"? Are you in pain or something?'

'Pain? I would suggest that pain is something you know nothing about!'

'I know a bit about it,' Tim said, rolling his shoulders. 'I had a bad toothache the other day.'

'Do not speak to me of such trifles.'
The man's steely grey eyes flashed with
contempt. 'Have you ever been speared
in your side by a hard-fisted Trojan and
watched your lifeblood trickle away? Do
you bear the scars of battle to this very
day, as testament to your suffering?'

'Um … no.'

'Then do not speak to me of pain.'

'All right.' Tim bent down to pick up
the vase. Sagging under the weight, he
took a few staggering steps along the
path. 'Bye.'

''

'Why do you keep saying that?' Tim
couldn't help asking.

'Your burden is light and yet you struggle. Show some determination.'

Tim nodded politely but decided to continue on his way. All he wanted to do was deliver the package. The sooner he finished, the sooner Hercules would be his friend again. 'Sorry, but I've gotta go.'

The man threw down his cup with a flourish. 'I did not fight the Trojan War to be snubbed by the likes of you.'

'The Trojan War?' Tim turned back. He'd read about that. It had all started because a beautiful woman called Helen had been kidnapped by some people called the Trojans. The Greeks had fought a war to bring her back.

'Indeed.' The man sighed. 'They do not make wars like that anymore.'

'Are you famous? Would I have heard of you?' Tim couldn't help getting interested.

'I should hope so! It was my clever plan that won the war.' The man sat up straighter. 'Build a wooden horse, conceal ourselves in its belly, and enter the gates of Troy. Odysseus the Cunning, some call me. Personally, I would have preferred Odysseus the Great.'

Tim stared at the powerful warrior sitting under the tree. 'You're Odysseus? Like, from *The Odyssey?* Wow!' he breathed. 'I love that story!'

'The what?'

'THE ODYSSEY!'

'That must be about me.' Odysseus puffed out his chest. 'I am not surprised that people are singing my praises.

After Troy fell, I voyaged over ten long years to reach my homeland. I experienced many fascinating adventures. It will take several days to relate them all to you.'

'I don't have several days.' Tim looked back at the path. 'I have to deliver this parcel.'

'I recall one time, when I was held captive by the beautiful nymph Calypso,' Odysseus continued as if Tim had not spoken. 'She was enthralled by my presence. Alas, I could not return her feelings. I yearned for my wife Penelope and could not bear to be away from her. I had to return to Ithaca. It took the intervention of the gods …'

There was no sign that the warrior was going to stop talking. Tim shifted anxiously from foot to foot. Hermes had said there'd be Hades to pay if the delivery was late. Tim didn't know quite what that meant, but he wasn't keen to find out. After ten awkward minutes, he decided to leave. As Odysseus wouldn't be quiet long enough for Tim to say goodbye, he simply waved. He hoisted up the vase, adjusted his grip on the parcel, and started walking.

Without breaking the flow of his story, Odysseus got up and joined him.

'Finally, the god Hermes was able to convince Calypso to release me. "It is not this man's destiny to stay with you forever," he told her. And then I …'

So long as he wasn't delayed, Tim didn't mind the company. It was an interesting story and it made the walk more enjoyable.

'I shall relieve you of your burden,' Odysseus said, after the vase began to slip from Tim's grasp for the third time. Odysseus held it easily in one hand. 'You have no stamina. Now, where was I? Oh, yes. As I was saying, Poseidon has never liked me. I was crossing the wine-dark sea when the ocean god became angered. He smashed my raft and …'

Eventually, Tim heard the gushing of a waterfall. Hermes had said that Narcissus could be found at a pool nearby. Encouraged, Tim walked faster. Soon the roar of falling water drowned out Odysseus' voice.

The warrior moved closer and shouted in Tim's ear. 'Have I mentioned the Land of the Lotus Eaters? The lazy inhabitants did nothing but eat. They shared with my men the fruit of the lotus, and eating it made them forget all about wanting to go home. My men wept bitterly when I was obliged to take them by force and–' Odysseus stopped talking abruptly.

Tim looked up to see what had made the warrior fall silent. It was the sight of a beautiful young man, barely out of his teens. He was sitting by the side of a still pond. He had long blonde ringlets, arched eyebrows and a delicate, almost feminine face.

'Narcissus?' Tim asked. The youth was staring into the pond and didn't reply. He matched Hermes' description exactly. Tim moved closer, in case he couldn't be heard over the sound of the waterfall. 'I've got a delivery for you.'

The young man didn't look up. Tim wondered why Narcissus was staring so intently at the pond. Had he dropped something in there? Tim walked up to him and followed his gaze. All he could see was the reflection of their faces.

'Excuse me,' he said.

'Mmm?' Narcissus stared dreamily at his image.

'I have to give you this package.'

'Package! package! package!'

Tim jumped as a girl ran out from the trees towards them, wringing her hands anxiously. Her long red hair was tangled, and her ragged green gown was stained with dirt. She must have been the one who had spoken.

'Sorry, it's not for you,' he said gently. He didn't want to upset the girl any further. She already looked distraught.

'YOU, YOU, YOU!'

she cried, pointing a trembling finger at Tim.

'Err, sure, it's me. I'll put it here, shall I?' Tim placed the package by the youth's side. Not tearing his eyes away from his reflection, Narcissus flapped a dismissive

hand. 'You need to open it, though,' Tim continued. 'Hermes said I can't leave until you do.'

'Doo-doo!' the girl cried, then clapped her hands over her mouth. Tim didn't think she'd meant to say that.

'Offer your thanks and open the parcel, oh long-haired youth,' Odysseus ordered.

Narcissus sighed but said nothing.

'You dishonour me,' the warrior snapped. 'I did not defeat Polyphemus, the one-eyed Cyclops, so that you could sigh at yourself. Stand up and open your parcel like a man.'

'So beautiful,' Narcissus murmured, ignoring Odysseus. 'I've never seen anyone lovelier. If only I could find someone that

matched my beauty, but alas …' He thrust
his face closer to the water.

'Alas!' the bedraggled girl cried, looking
at Tim imploringly.

'Sorry, but who's she?' Tim had to ask.

Narcissus finally looked up. 'Oh, her?
She's Echo. Bit dull. All she does is repeat
what you say. It's some sort of curse,
apparently.' Yawning, he turned back to his
reflection.

'Curse! Curse!' Echo repeated
frantically.

'I think she's trying to tell me
something,' Tim said, peering at her face.

'Something!' Echo nodded vigorously.

'Well, what?'

'What, what, what?' Echo echoed.

Stamping her foot in frustration, she pointed at the package.

Echo was behaving really strangely, Tim thought. The package wasn't even for her. Why was she so curious about it? Tim turned back to Narcissus. 'Look, I'll open it for you.' The youth ignored him.

Tim squatted down and picked up the parcel. It was wrapped in a coarse cloth and tied with string. He eased off the fabric and found a polished wooden box inside. It glimmered in the sunlight.

'You, you, you!' Echo cried, lunging forward and gripping Tim's arm.

'That's right.' He shook her hand off gently. 'I'll do it.'

'Do it!' She shouted in his face, spittle spraying his cheek.

Tim wiped his face and turned back to the box. Her curse may have prevented her saying so exactly, but it didn't take a genius to see that she was desperate for him to open it. He flipped a metal clasp and the lid came up smoothly. Inside the box was a sleek black object. It looked a lot like the oil flask that Hera had had made to trap Tim inside. There was a picture of him on it, he recalled.

This one was blank, which was odd. Most flasks were decorated. Maybe there was something on the other side. A picture of Narcissus, perhaps. Tim could easily imagine the vain youth wanting an ancient selfie. Curious, he gripped the flask and flipped it over. A tingling sensation flooded up his hands and along his arms. It was as if a very mild electric current flowed through him. Not painful, but not pleasant either.

It wasn't the tingle that made Tim drop the flask in horror, though. It was what he saw on its other side.

The all-too-familiar picture of himself holding the time-travelling vase.

It was the same flask as the one in the
British Museum! The one the Titan
Epimetheus had made, unaware of Hera's
plans. The flask had kept turning up in
Tim's home, in places where he might
accidentally brush against it. He had
spotted Hermes fluttering around at
the time. When Tim had mentioned it,
Hermes claimed he'd been moving the
flask out of the way, trying to protect him.

Zoe, however, was certain that Hermes had planted it.

The tingling sensation flooded through Tim's body and down his legs. He dropped the flask, but it was too late. Its effect was spreading.

Suddenly, the world around him seemed to grow. The pebbles turned into boulders, the scraggly bushes into soaring trees. The flask loomed over him, as big as a building. Tim knew what it meant. He was shrinking.

'No!' he cried, his voice high-pitched and squeaky. He sounded like a cartoon mouse.

'No! No!' Echo shouted. Maybe she'd been trying to warn him about the flask!

If only he'd tried harder to understand her.

Just as suddenly, the world stopped growing. The tingling was replaced by a loud roaring. It sounded like the waterfall, but louder. The air around him whooshed upwards in powerful, swirling gusts. Tim's hair stood on end. It felt like a giant vacuum cleaner was hovering over his head, ready to scoop him up.

'Argh!' he shouted as he felt himself rise into the air. He was floating! The cushion of air drifted him closer to the flask's lip. He peddled his legs as if he were riding an invisible bicycle. Tim realised what was happening but was powerless to stop it. He could hear Echo wailing. 'Odysseus!' Tim squeaked.

Before the warrior could react, Tim felt himself drop. He plummeted downwards, straight into the flask, and hit the bottom with a *thunk*. Dazed, he pulled himself gingerly to his feet. The interior of the flask was smooth and slippery and curved. There was no way he could climb out.

'Hey! Get me out!' Tim hammered on the wall with his fists.

'Out, out, out!'

Tim felt the flask being lifted. He thrust his hands to the side to steady himself. The sky was blotted out as a steely grey eye peered inside. It glimmered with scorn.

'It is as I feared.' Odysseus' rumbling voice echoed in the narrow flask. 'Laziness. This is most distressing.'

'What? No!' cried Tim.

'I sensed that perhaps you might be made of sterner stuff. That you might even have the makings of a hero … but no. Here you are

languishing
in a lekythos,
rather than doing
an honest day's
work.'

'I didn't ask to be
in here!' Tim called. 'I
was trapped!'

'How so? Did the song of
the Sirens lure you down there?

Then I would have you plug your ears with beeswax as I did my men.'

'It wasn't sirens,' Tim protested. 'Don't they live by sea?'

'Exactly,' said Odysseus. 'Therefore you are simply being lazy.'

'No, I—'

'I am going back to sit under my tree. Perhaps I shall meet another, worthier traveller. One who will appreciate my tales and learn from my example. I have heard rumours of a bard who is said to relish feats of bravery and adventure ...'

Tim felt the flask being lowered. 'No. Wait!' he cried. It was no use. Tim felt the ground vibrate as the warrior stalked away.

'Stop shouting,' Narcissus complained. 'All this noise is distracting me. How am I supposed to admire my reflection?'

'Please!' Tim begged. 'I'm trapped.'

'Trapped,' Echo moaned.

'Echo, can you help me?'

'Me, me, me.'

Tim guessed not. 'Narcissus?'

'Not my problem,' came the sulky reply. 'Be quiet, or I'll throw you and your stupid flask into the waterfall.'

Tim gulped. That was all he needed. He dropped his head in his hands and wondered whether Hermes had known the oil flask was in the parcel. But how could he? The messenger god had shown him several packages, this just happened to be one of them. And he only gave it to Tim because it was small and marked "Urgent".

Still, it made no difference. Whether Hermes was involved or not, Tim was stuck. A lump rose in his throat. The only people able to help him had no idea who he was. Even if they suddenly remembered him, Hercules and Zoe didn't know where he was, or that he was trapped.

Groaning, he sank onto the flask's flat, narrow base. All around the constant roar of the waterfall bounced and magnified, until Tim covered his ears with both hands. He stared upwards, his eyes tracing the curve of the flask's sides, thinking how nice it would be to have some beeswax earplugs after all.

Of course! The wax plug! During
a previous adventure, Epimetheus had
promised to insert a hole in the flask. He
had been outraged when he learnt of
Hera's plans to trap Tim. The hole would
allow Tim to climb out and escape if Hera
ever managed to trap him. The Titan said
he would seal the hole carefully with wax,

making it invisible to the eye. All Tim had
to do was find it!

Tim sprang to his feet. He ran his
hands eagerly over the walls. If the plug
was there, he should be able to feel it.
Tim hoped the Titan had the sense to put
the hole low down, not up high where he
couldn't reach. After a few minutes his
search became more desperate. The walls
of the flask were smooth and uniform.
Tim's stomach dropped. He couldn't feel
the plug.

Tim's heart began to pound.

'Calm down,' he murmured. 'Don't panic.
It must be here. Epimetheus promised.
I'll try again.' He had to be methodical.
More slowly this time, he started from the

bottom and slid his hands up as far as he could reach. When he finished with one section, he started on another.

There. Tim's hands snagged on something. He tried again, just to be sure. Yes, the texture of the wall was different in one spot. There was a very slight lump where the wax had collected. Experimenting, he scratched at it with his fingernails. Small layers of wax peeled off. *Yes!*

Now all he had to do was light a match, hold it to the plug and melt the wax. Brilliant! Except there was one problem.

He didn't have any matches.

Tim hadn't realised it would be so hard
to get hold of a box of matches. Mum
kept a few boxes for lighting candles, but
she'd refused to let him have one. She still
believed he'd burnt their garden, way back
when Hercules had taken a torch to the
weeds, attacking them as if they were the
Hydra. Tim had also tried asking Larry.
He too refused. Larry thought Tim was
putting himself in too much danger. 'If

you don't go back to Ancient Greece, you won't get trapped in the first place,' the teacher had said.

Tim had given up. If only they'd trusted him! He would have been able to melt the wax plug and escape.

Maybe he could scratch his way out. He tried using his fingernails again, but it didn't get him far. It hurt, too. Tim emptied out his jeans pockets to see if he had anything that would help. A balled-up tissue, a packet of mints, some string, an interesting pebble, and a Golden Fleece glove. *The glove!*

Tim pulled it on and waited. He expected to grow so fast the flask shattered into pieces around him. Nothing happened. He waited a bit more. Still nothing. He stayed as small as ever. Was that because Zoe had the other half of the pair, and you needed both to undo a shrinking curse? Perhaps there simply wasn't enough fleece in one glove to do the trick.

Tim was out of ideas.

He decided to sit down and rest for a while. All the events of the day – the adventure with Jason, coming home to discover Mum wanted to sell the vase, going straight back to see Zoe, being forgotten, delivering the parcel – had left him exhausted. It was hard to believe all that had happened in one day. Sailing the seas to fetch Hippocrates so the doctor could heal Zoe felt like ages ago, but for him it had been just that morning.

No wonder he was out of ideas. Maybe a nap … a little one … just to refresh his brain … his tired eyes … and while he was at it, the rest of him …

■　　■　　■

When Tim next opened his eyes, the view from the oil flask's opening was different. He could still see trees, but the angle had changed. He became aware of a rocking motion. The flask bobbed gently, like a sailing ship on calm waters. Someone had picked the flask up and was carrying it away.

Tim sprang to his feet. He wasn't sure how long he'd been asleep. He opened his mouth to call out, then shut it again. Was that wise? He didn't know who had picked the flask up. It might be a thief! Or worse – it might be Hera. Then again, he had nothing to gain by remaining silent. His only hope of escape was to shout, and hope someone would let him out.

'Hey!' he called. 'Can you hear me?' The person carrying the flask stopped walking for a moment. Encouraged, Tim shouted again. 'I'm in here!'

'Strange,' said a crackly voice. 'I thought I heard something. Must be imagining it.' Whoever it was resumed walking.

'You didn't,' Tim said. 'I need your help.'

'Probably a wood nymph,' the voice said, then snorted. 'Hmph. I hate nymphs. They play havoc with my geraniums.'

It was then that Tim realised who it was. It had to be Perseus, the extremely old hero who had once slain the snake-haired Medusa. He was a fanatical gardener and Zoe's great-great-grandfather. Now retired from hero work, he lived in a cave and spent all his time tending to his flowers.

'I'm not a wood nymph!' Tim called. 'I'm Tim Baker.'

'That's what they all say,' Perseus said sternly. 'I know a nymph when I hear one. And don't think I don't know who dug those holes in my flower beds. No point denying it.'

'But–'

'But nothing. I know what you're after. You want to stop me taking this flask.' Tim stumbled as Perseus waved the flask around. 'Well, too bad. It's mine – I found it. I walked all the way up to the waterfall to look for a rare species of orchid, and I saw it. Someone must have thrown it away.'

'You can have the flask,' Tim gasped. 'Just let me out!'

Perseus hobbled faster. 'I know your game. Talk the old geezer into putting down the flask, then snatch it and run away. Oh yes, I'm onto you.'

'No, I–'

'Well forget it, wherever you are,' Perseus continued. 'I'm hanging onto this. It'll make a lovely pot for my long-stemmed roses.'

Tim realised there was no point arguing. He just had to hope that when Perseus popped his roses in the flask, Tim could climb the stems and escape. Unless the aged hero put the water in first …

… but that was something Tim would rather not think about.

7

The light above the flask opening
suddenly grew dim. Shifting shadows
flickered and danced. That meant
Perseus had entered his cave, Tim
realised. The shadows were cast by
the blazing torches he kept on the
walls. It was in this cave that Hera had
recently trapped Tim, Zoe and Hercules,
and Zoe's legs had been crushed by a
boulder as they tried to escape.

The old man started humming a cheerful tune. 'Lovely,' he murmured. 'Lovely little pot for my red roses.'

Tim felt the flask judder. Perseus must have put it down. Tim was just thinking that he ought to try calling out again, when he heard a voice that made him fall silent.

'Hello, Grandpa.' It was Zoe!

'Well, well, another visit so soon.' The aged hero sounded pleased. 'And how is my favourite great-great-granddaughter?'

'I'm fine, thank you. How are you?'

Tim thought it was odd that Zoe hadn't mentioned that she had been imprisoned and injured in this very cave just a few hours ago. Had she forgotten that too? How was that possible?

'A column snapped and a boulder fell in my back room, but other than that, everything's fine,' Perseus replied. 'Have a look at my new flower pot. I found it today while I was out orchid hunting.'

Tim heard Zoe's footsteps coming nearer. 'It's nice,' she agreed. Her voice was now loud and clear. 'What's that drawing on the front?'

'Probably some type of monster,' Perseus said, not sounding particularly interested.

'No … I don't think so.' Tim saw a shadow fall as Zoe leant closer and blocked out some of the light. 'It looks like a boy. But why is he wearing such strange clothes?'

'Like I said, it's probably a monster.'

Zoe was silent for a moment. 'He doesn't look like a monster.' Her voice sounded doubtful. 'He looks ... friendly.'

Tim tensed. He was tempted to call out but he didn't want to frighten her off.

'A mythical creature, then,' Perseus said dismissively. 'Anyway, to what do I owe the pleasure of this visit? Did that muscle-headed father of yours send you?'

'Oh right,' Zoe said, her shadow receding. 'No, Mum sent me. I've brought you some fruit. It's amazing.'

'Amazing fruit? Let me see.' Tim heard rustling, and then a startled, 'You're not eating those!'

'Why not?' Zoe asked. 'They're delicious. Dad can't get enough of them.'

'Throw them away,' Perseus said, 'as fast as you can. Actually, no. Not near here. I don't want the seeds to take root in my garden.'

'But why?' Zoe asked. 'What's the matter with them?'

'They are the fruit of all evil! Who gave them to you?'

'Hera. She said they were a peace offering.'

Tim felt his blood run cold. Now things were starting to make sense: Hera was involved. Tim still didn't know what had happened, but maybe he was about to find out.

'Why would she need to give a peace offering?' Perseus asked. Despite his advanced age, his voice sounded sharp.

'I'm not sure,' Zoe admitted. 'I wasn't really listening. Dad seemed to think what she said was okay, though.'

'Your father!' Perseus said scornfully. 'He would think anything was fine if it meant he could fill his stomach.'

'They must've had some sort of fight. I don't know what it was about.'

'Tch.' Perseus clicked his tongue. 'Did you eat any?'

'We all did.' Zoe sounded worried. 'Why, what's wrong with them?'

'Nothing so simple, my dear. That is the fruit of the lotus, from the Land of the

Lotus Eaters. Eat them and you lose your memory.'

Tim recalled Odysseus' story about his men eating the fruit. Now he understood. Hera had deliberately destroyed his friends' memory of him!

'But I haven't,' Zoe protested. 'I know my name, I know yours …'

'Is there nothing you've forgotten?'

'No! I don't know. Maybe I don't remember that I can't remember!' Zoe said.

'Very likely,' the aged hero cackled. 'Now think. Has anything odd happened since eating the fruit?'

'Well … last night a strange boy came to our house. He was wearing very odd clothes,' Zoe paused, 'just like that picture on your flask. He seemed to know who we were, but Dad and I didn't recognise him. Dad threw him out.'

She was talking about Tim! This had to be the right time. Tim took a deep breath. 'Hey Zoe, in here!'

'What was that?' she yelped. 'I heard a voice.'

'It sounds like that wood nymph.' Perseus exhaled sharply. 'Don't tell me it's followed me home. Keep away from my begonias!' he bellowed. His voice echoed off the cave walls.

'It came from your flower pot …'

'It's me! Tim Baker, your friend. Look in the flask and you'll see.' A shadow fell over him and what little light remained was blotted out. Tim saw a gigantic eye loom above him. 'We've had adventures together,' he said, desperate to convince her. 'Your father is Hercules and your mum is Agatha.'

The eye blinked.

'Perseus should know who I am! You've got to get me out of here,' Tim continued. 'Let me out and I'll explain everything.'

Zoe moved away and the light flooded back into the flask. 'Grandpa … there's something inside.'

'Tip it out,' Perseus said. 'I don't want anything to interfere with my roses.'

'Be gentle when you turn it–' The rest of Tim's sentence was drowned out by a loud yowling. Tim felt as if someone had emptied a bucket of iced water down his spine. He knew that sound too well.

It was Hera's peacocks. Whenever they turned up, the goddess was sure to follow.

Sure enough, within seconds Tim heard Hera's silky voice. 'My petals,' she said, using the nauseating name she called her peacocks, 'you found the flask. Good birds. There'll be some extra treats in your feed tonight.'

Tim heard the peacocks coo like doves. He knew how vicious they could be, however, and the sound made him shudder.

'You keep those rotten birds off my flowers,' Perseus grumbled. 'I don't want their big beaks in my begonias.'

'How dare you speak to me like that!' Hera said. 'I am your queen. Kneel before me.'

'Not with these old knees,' Perseus said. 'They stopped working decades ago.'

'Then – old man – hand me that flask. It is mine. You have stolen it.'

'I didn't steal it, I found it.' Perseus sounded sulky. 'Some fool left it near a pond. I rescued it.'

'Your queen commands you.' Tim heard Hera's gown rustle as she spoke.

'Why do you want it, anyway?' Zoe was bold enough to ask. 'It's just an old flask.'

'Oh, it's you.' Hera sounded irritated. 'You do not recognise the picture on it?'

'Should I?' Zoe asked.

'Of course not.' The goddess paused, and then her tone changed. 'Did you eat some of that delicious fruit I gave you, dear child?'

'I did,' Zoe answered promptly.

'I am so glad to hear it. Was it nice?' The goddess' voice was sickly sweet. 'Did you feel … different after you ate it?'

'Yes,' Zoe replied

'In what way?'

'It gave me the runs.'

'Really.' Hera's voice sharpened again. 'Well, I cannot waste my time in this grubby cave. Hand me my flask or suffer the consequences.'

❧❧

'No. It's mine,' Perseus said.

Tim felt the flask being roughly hoisted into the air. He thrust out his hands to steady himself. The flask came to an abrupt halt as it bumped against something hard. He looked up and saw the underside of Perseus' withered chin. Tim realised he was clasping the flask to his chest.

'I want it for my long-stemmed roses.'

'Roses? You fool. My need is far greater than yours.'

'Why? What do you want it for?' Zoe piped up again. Tim could picture the girl tossing her long ringlets in that defiant way of hers.

'My business is no concern of yours,' Hera snapped. 'Now give it to me, old man. Or I will prise it from your arthritic fingers and your punishment shall be severe.'

'OH REALLY? WELL THEN COME AND GET IT!'

For a moment, the aged hero's voice boomed like a Spartan king's.

'I will!' Hera cried.

Tim felt the flask being tugged this way and that. He gripped his stomach as it leapt and lurched. It was like being tossed about in a boat during a violent storm. He felt bruises spring up on his arms and legs as he bounced from wall to wall. 'Stop it!' he squawked, but

didn't think they could hear him over their bickering.

Then, all of a sudden, the motion changed.

'Hey!' Perseus said.

Tim felt himself moving in one direction – very fast.

'Bring that back, you cursed child!' That was Hera.

Tim could hear puffing and panting. He looked up but all he could see was the blue sky and some fluffy white clouds racing by. 'Zoe?' he asked. 'Is that you?'

'Well of course it is, whoever you are,' she said between breaths. 'Do you think the others can run this fast?' She kept running.

'Ma! Dad!' Zoe called out as she burst through her front door. 'I've got to show you something.'

'You've got to show us what?' Tim heard Hercules ask.

'Not a what. A who!' Tim felt himself rise as Zoe held up the oil flask.

'Zoe.' Hercules' voice was firm. 'You're holding a lekythos. That's not a who, it's a what. Agatha, why did you not teach this child to speak properly?'

Tim heard footsteps, then Agatha's calm and measured voice. 'What's this about, dear? Did you give Grandpa the fruit?'

'Yes. No! I mean, I took it,' Zoe said, 'but he sent it back. I've got it here.'

'Why didn't he take it?' Agatha sounded concerned. 'It's full of vitamins.'

'Ma, he told me it's the fruit of the lotus. Do you know what that is?'

'I do,' Hercules said. 'It is delicious! Give it to me, I will eat it.'

'Wait,' Agatha said, alarmed. 'Zoe, are you sure? It cannot be lotus. We have not forgotten anything.'

'I have certainly not forgotten how to eat it!' Hercules boomed, smacking his lips. 'Hand it over.'

'Husband, we have heard of the fruit of the lotus,' Agatha said slowly. 'Your friend Odysseus told us the tale. Do you recall? He went to the Land of the Lotus Eaters and his men ate the fruit. They forgot all about their mission. They became listless and lazy and didn't want to leave. Odysseus had to remove them by force.'

'Hmm. Yes. I know the story. He has told it many, many times,' Hercules said. His voice became doubtful. 'Can this really be such an evil fruit? It tastes so good!'

'That is often the way,' Agatha sighed. Her sigh was like the one Tim's mother made when she stopped herself eating another chocolate.

'It cannot be …' Hercules sounded upset. 'Hera gave us that fruit. My father's wife is like a mother to me. She would never do anything to harm our family.'

'Dad! She was mean to Great-great-grandad! She shouted at him. She was furious. She threatened to punish him if he didn't do what she wanted.'

'Wha—'

'And I think she's trapped someone in this.' Zoe waved the flask around and Tim had to sit down to stop his head from spinning.

'What do you mean?' Agatha asked.

'I mean,' Zoe said with relish in her voice, 'there's a boy inside! He says he knows us.'

'What?' Hercules roared. 'Not that strange boy who keeps coming to our door?'

'It must be. He looked just like the picture on this flask,' Zoe said. 'Weird clothes, pale skin, snub nose, weak chin, knobbly knees—'

Tim felt that it was time to object. 'Oi! I can hear you, you know.'

'What was that?' Hercules sounded

startled. 'Some kind of wood nymph?'

'That's the boy in the flask,' Zoe said.

'It cannot be.' Hercules was certain.
'Boys don't have such high voices.
Captured wood nymphs will say anything
to be released, Zoe. Don't listen to them.'

'I'm not a wood
nymph,' Tim found
himself saying yet
again, trying to make his
tiny voice deeper. 'I'm
Tim Baker! Look in the
flask and you'll see.'

A sparkling black
eye covered the flask's
opening. Tim heard a
deep intake of breath.

'You are right, Zoe.' Hercules pulled away and shook his head. 'It *is* that strange boy! Quick, fetch a cloth. We must make a stopper and seal the flask.'

'Why, Dad?'

'For him to be trapped like that, he must have been up to no good. Perhaps Hera put him in there to protect you.'

'How can he harm our daughter?' Agatha asked peering into the vase. 'He is just a child. It's cruel to leave him in there. We must get him out and give him a chance to tell his story.'

Hercules hesitated. 'If you say so. But I must warn you: at the first sign of trouble I will eject him onto the street.' The hero tipped the flask upside down and shook it.

'Not like tha–' Agatha started to say, but she was too late.

Tim tumbled head over heels in the confined space. He flipped over so fast, his stomach jumped into his throat. Finally, his bottom wedged itself firmly in the flask's opening. Like a cork in a bottle, Tim was stuck.

'Mmpf,' he said, his head and legs dangling uselessly.

'Well, that didn't work.'

Tim felt something pressing on his backside – probably Hercules' thumb – and he slammed back to the bottom of the flask.

'There's a wax plug in the side,' Tim croaked, winded by the fall. 'Melt it.'

'Dad, can you bring a flaming torch?'

'Good idea. It is rather dark in here.' Hercules' voice got quieter as he walked away. The room brightened when he returned a few moments later. 'Here it is.'

'Hold it near the flask,' Zoe said. 'Hey, strange boy, where's the plug?'

'Here,' he called, rapping on the flask wall with his knuckles.

'All right. Stand back.'

Tim pressed himself against the far wall. The light from the torch intensified as the temperature skyrocketed. Beads of sweat broke out on Tim's brow. He hoped the wax would melt quickly, before he did. Now he knew how roast chickens felt!

Tim squinted at the plug. Nothing seemed to be happening. He blinked and then part of the wall started to shimmer and glow.

'ITS WORKING!'

Zoe cried. 'Hold it there, Dad.'

Tim watched as the side of the flask bulged and trickled. A puddle of hot wax pooled on the flask floor and he inched away from it. The heat was becoming unbearable. It was hard to breathe, and he could feel his eyebrows start to singe.

'That will do,' he heard Agatha say. 'Remove the torch. Give him a chance to climb out.'

The light faded, but the molten wax continued to spread, hissing and seething like lava, getting closer to his feet. Tim sized up the hole in the flask, squatted, and hurled himself over the bubbling pool. He sailed through the scorched air and out into the light. A delicious coolness washed over him. It was the most wonderful feeling until …

Thud.

Tim bounced off the end of a table and plummeted to the floor. At first it seemed like a very long way down. But as he fell, he grew larger. Hera's spell was reversing!

By the time he reached the ground, he was back to full size.

'Ow,' he groaned. His body was covered with bruises. How would he explain them to Mum?

Tim stood up shakily and gripped the edge of the table to steady himself.

'You're not trying to sell us an amphora, are you?' Hercules eyed him suspiciously.

'No. I'm your friend, I promise.'

Zoe, Hercules and Agatha stared at Tim, then at each other.

'Sorry, child, we don't remember,' Agatha said. 'It's not that we don't believe you, but …' She let the rest of her sentence hang in the air.

Tim frowned. How could he convince them? 'Err … I know! You once made a chiton for me. You must still have it. If I can find it …'

'I make lots of clothes,' Agatha said, shaking her head. 'How does showing me a chiton that I made prove that I made it for you?'

Tim wished the Greeks had iron-on name labels like they did back home. 'Well, how about this?' He pulled the Golden Fleece glove out of his pocket and waved it in the air. 'Remember, Zoe? We've got one each.'

'Anyone can own a glove,' Zoe said, unimpressed.

'Not these gloves. They're special.'

'So you say.' Zoe pulled a face.

'They're made of the Golden Fleece. There are only two in the whole wide world.'

'Don't be silly. Who'd make gloves out of the Golden Fleece?'

'Arachne. Remember her? Giant spider?' Tim raised his fingers to his mouth in imitation of fangs.

'Ew!' Zoe shuddered and took a step backwards. 'A giant spider that makes gloves? You're off your rocker.'

'I am not! Ask Hermes. Ask Perseus. They'd know!'

Agatha patted Tim on the arm. 'I'm sure you're telling us the truth – or at least you think you are. But you look exhausted. Sit down and have something to eat.'

At the mention of food, Tim's stomach gurgled greedily. 'Maybe a quick snack,' he agreed. 'I'm starving.'

'Would you like some fruit?' Zoe asked, grinning.

Hoping for some figs or grapes, Tim returned her grin. 'Yes please,' he said. The smile disappeared when he saw her hold out the fruit of the lotus. 'Very funny.'

Tim wolfed down a thick soup made of dried beans and vegetables. 'This is great. Thank you.'

'What did you say your name was?' Head tilted like a sparrow, Zoe looked at him through bright eyes.

'Tim. Tim Baker.' He gazed across the table at his friend, willing her to remember him.

'Tim-tim-baker?' Hercules shook his

head. 'That cannot be a real name. Surely you made that up as well.'

'My first name is Tim and my last name is Baker.' They didn't have surnames in Ancient Greece, which was why nearly everyone here called him "Tim Baker", as if it were one name.

'Two names!' Hercules' eyes widened. 'You must be very important. Are you a god from a foreign land?'

'Is that why you dress funny?' Zoe asked.

'Zoe! We don't make personal remarks,' Agatha said as she refilled Tim's bowl.

'No, I'm a boy from the future. See this fabric?'

Tim tugged at his T-shirt. 'Polyester doesn't get invented for ages. Also, I come from another country. It's called England.'

'Never heard of it.' Zoe was adamant.

'Well, you wouldn't have. The Romans knew about us, but I'm not sure about the Greeks.'

'England? Romans? Polywhoster? None of those things exist.' Hercules sniffed. 'Are you perhaps of feeble mind?'

Tim felt tears prickle at his eyes. 'That's exactly what you said when we first met. Back then I didn't believe in Greek gods and heroes, and now – now you don't believe in me.'

'Tell us everything,' Agatha suggested, 'from the beginning.'

Tim nodded. He took a deep breath and then started talking. He told them about the magic vase, and the spells, and the adventures. He glossed over the dangerous bits – no point in upsetting Hercules all over again. Finally, he got to the part about his mother wanting to sell the vase.

'So … err … that's why I came by,' Tim added. 'To explain why I might not return. I didn't want you to think I'd forgotten you.'

'And instead, we have forgotten you,' Agatha said, her face grave.

Tim shrugged. 'Yeah, well. You can't help it.' He looked at Zoe and her parents, their faces rosy in the flickering torchlight. Over the past few weeks, Tim had come to think of them as his second family. 'So, do you believe me?' He crossed his fingers under the table.

Hercules and Zoe hesitated, but Agatha nodded. 'I do. You seem to be a decent, honest boy. I cannot believe you would make this up. Why would you?'

'Maybe because he's barking mad,' Zoe muttered. 'But *if* it's all true,' she added hastily before she could be reprimanded, 'we have to stop his mother from selling the vase.'

'GOOD IDEA!'

Hercules slapped the table and a crack zigzagged out from under his palm. 'I will chain her to a cliff until she changes her mind. That ought to do it.'

'You can't do that!' Tim squeaked, jumping up in alarm. 'She's a good person. She's the best mother anyone could ask for!'

'He won't. Don't worry.' Agatha put a gentle hand on Tim's shoulder and pressed him back down into his chair. 'I think you need to talk with your mother. She only wants what's best for you.'

'She does.' Tim sighed. 'That's the trouble.'

Agatha looked unperturbed. 'Return home, child. Sometimes mothers understand more than you know. She might surprise you.'

Nodding sadly, Tim turned to get his vase. It wasn't where he normally left it: in the corner, covered by a piece of cloth. He frowned. He looked around but couldn't see it.

'It's not here!' he said. 'Of course! I couldn't leave it here before, so I took it with me. All the way to the waterfall! That's so far.' He groaned at the thought of the difficult walk ahead of him. He was exhausted, covered in bruises, and upset that his friends still didn't remember him. He didn't have it in him to walk all that way.

'It doesn't have to be that far,' Hercules said, stroking his beard. 'Not many people know this, but there is a shortcut. Once, when I was bored, I dug a tunnel through the mountain. You can use that.'

'I'm going with him.' Zoe shook out her curls and stood next to Tim, ready to set off.

'Oh no you shall not—' Hercules started, but wilted under his wife's glare. 'All right, then,' he said reluctantly. 'Just this one time. Then you shall return through the tunnel as fast as you can – or I will come looking for you!'

■ ■ ■

Hercules was right. The trip was much shorter when you could cut through the centre of the mountain. After a quick and easy walk, the secret passage rose steeply upwards, ending in a narrow crevice. It was a relief to leave the confined gloominess of the tunnel – which felt too much like the interior of the flask for Tim's liking. Leading the way, Tim scrambled out into the sunlight. The sound of running water filled the air and

a fine spray wet his cheeks. The waterfall was only metres away.

'The pond is down there.' Tim had to shout to be heard over the roaring water. 'That's where I left the vase.'

With Zoe close on his heels, Tim strode quickly towards the pond. If his adventures were about to end anyway, there was no point dragging things out. But when he reached the spot he came to a standstill. The vase was nowhere to be seen.

Narcissus was still there, looking at his reflection and sighing.

'Hey, um, Narcissus,' Tim said. 'I was here earlier. Remember me?'

'Mmm?' came the dreamy reply.

'There was a vase there.' Tim pointed at the spot. 'Do you know where it went?'

'Mmm, don't know. Don't care.'

'Look,' Zoe snapped, her temper flaring. 'How can you not know? Weren't you here all this time? Are you blind or something?'

'There's no point.' Tim waved her away. 'All he ever does is stare at himself.'

'Ew, that's creepy.'

'Where's Echo? Is she still here?' Tim asked, looking around. Maybe the bedraggled girl knew what had happened to the vase. Not that she'd be able to tell them!

Narcissus shrugged.

'Hang on. You've seen Echo?' Zoe asked, spinning around to face Tim.

'Yeah. I think she was trying to warn me about the flask, but I couldn't understand her.'

'Hmm. Maybe you *are* telling the truth.' Zoe tugged thoughtfully at her curls. 'Once when Hera was trying to spy on Zeus, Echo distracted her at the worst possible moment with endless chatter. Hera was so furious that she punished Echo. She made her only able to repeat other people's words. Echo was so upset she hid herself away, but I've heard she sometimes appears to warn others when Hera's on the warpath.'

'I hope Hera hasn't got my vase.' Tim gulped as the thought occurred to him. 'Zoe, you'd better go home, or your dad will worry.'

'No chance.' Zoe pressed her lips together. 'I'm not missing out on an adventure.'

Tim grinned. She might not remember him, but she hadn't changed a bit. Maybe they could become friends all over again.

'Hey, strange boy, what's that?' Zoe's change of tone was abrupt.

'What's what?'

'That.' Zoe pointed over Tim's shoulder, her eyes widening. 'Am I going mad – or is that a lion?'

11

'A lion?' Tim scoffed. 'You're having me on. I'm not actually feeble minded, you know.'

Zoe clicked her tongue impatiently. 'It's over there. Look!'

Tim followed her outstretched finger and his heart leapt into his throat. 'Whoa! How did that get there?'

'How would I know? Do you want me to go and ask it?'

'Sssh. I think it's seen us!'

And indeed, the lion did seem to be watching them. Its yellow eyes stared unblinkingly in their direction. It opened its mouth in a giant yawn, rose to its feet and shook out its mane.

'It's going to pounce,' Tim hissed, tensing himself to run.

Instead, the lion turned in the opposite direction. It took a few sedate paces, then twisted around so that it could look over its shoulder at them.

'I think it wants us to follow it,' Zoe said.

'Don't be ridiculous. It wants to eat us.'

'Then it would come charging, wouldn't it?' Zoe tugged at Tim's sleeve, dragging him forwards. 'I think it wants to show us something.'

Tim dug his heels in. 'Yeah. Its starving children, waiting at home for their lunch.'

'Come on!' Zoe stepped cautiously towards the lion. Seemingly satisfied, the majestic beast nodded before turning and plodding along a rough tree-lined path.

Sighing, Tim followed, his muscles tensed to make a quick getaway.

After ten minutes of walking, he had to

admit that Zoe was right. The lion was showing no aggression towards them. Rather, it cast concerned looks in their direction, as if it were checking that they were keeping up. Tim felt like he'd stumbled into Narnia.

'All I need is some Turkish Delight,' he muttered.

'Some what?'

'Never mind,' Tim said. 'How long are we going to do this for? I've got to find the vase.'

'This must be important or else why—Oh, wow.' Zoe stopped walking abruptly and Tim bumped into her. 'Look at that!' she breathed.

The path wound through a thick cluster of trees and ended in a small clearing. At the far end stood a large, elegant building. It was surrounded by a garden filled with flowers, graceful statues and fountains. Most astonishing of all, however, were the wild animals that paced to and fro. More than a dozen lions, bears and wolves strolled freely through the garden. Tim couldn't believe his eyes.

The lion they'd followed walked up a set of marble steps to the house's front door and sank onto its haunches. With a heavy sigh, it rested its head on its front paws. It stared at the children unblinkingly.

'It's telling us to go inside,' Zoe said.

Tim had read too many fairy tales to simply walk up to a strange house in the woods and knock on the door. He shook his head. 'I don't like gingerbread,' he said, by way of explanation.

'You *are* barking mad,' Zoe decided.

'Maybe,' Tim said wryly. 'Can you blame me? This whole thing is impossible. Why would a lion want us to go into a house?'

'Maybe your vase is in there. Have you thought of that?'

Tim hadn't. Now that he did, he had to admit that it was a possibility. In any case, he couldn't leave without finding out. But what if the whole thing was a trap set by Hera?

That thought seemed to have occurred to Zoe as well. 'I think you should go up and knock. I'll stay near the path in case I need to run for help,' she said.

Tim nodded. He couldn't come up with a better plan. 'Okay. Make sure you keep out of sight.' With a final disbelieving glance at the not-so-wild animals, Tim walked up to the grand house. The lion shifted to make way for him. Holding his breath, Tim knocked.

The door opened smoothly. A beautiful young woman with flowing golden hair stood in the doorway. Her soft blue eyes shone, and her face lit up in a delighted smile. It reminded Tim of sunshine on a spring day. He suddenly felt unusually shy.

'Ah, err, um,' he stumbled, trying to untie his tongue.

'Yes, my sweet? What a nice young man. What can I do for you?' The woman's voice was hypnotic, like waves washing gently onto a beach.

'Err … ah. I've lost it.'

The woman arched a delicate eyebrow. 'Lost what, my precious?'

'M-my vase. That's it. I've lost my vase. It's very important,' he found himself telling her. 'It's magic!'

'Is it indeed? You must be very special.'

Tim puffed out his chest, agreeing that he was.

'So, um, I was wondering whether you've got it. Like, maybe someone brought it here?' He felt it didn't matter awfully much if she didn't have it. It was enough just to bask in that lovely smile. He would have been happy to stand there and stare at her all day long.

'As a matter of fact, I do have it. Would you like to come inside and see?'

Tim didn't need to be asked twice.

12

Without a backwards glance, Tim crossed the threshold. He entered a broad hallway, lit by the rosy glow of dozens of candles. The delicious odour of cooking drifted from the rear of the house. Even though Tim had just eaten, the food smelt so good his stomach rumbled.

'Are you hungry, my angel? Come and have something to eat before you go.'

'If you like,' Tim said, trying to play it cool. He told himself that he didn't want to offend this kind woman by taking his vase and leaving abruptly.

'Your vase is in the dining area,' she said, sweeping down the hallway. 'Follow me.'

The smell grew stronger and Tim's mouth watered. 'How did you get it?' he asked. He didn't want to just eat and leave either, in case it was impolite.

'A warrior came to the door with it. He offered to exchange the vase for a chance to tell me his life story.' She smiled. 'I took pity on him and threw a good meal into the bargain.' She suddenly stopped and turned around. 'But, oh dear, where are my manners?

We haven't introduced ourselves. My name is Circe.'

'Sir-see,' Tim said dreamily. 'What a lovely name. It sounds like birds singing at dawn.' His cheeks turned bright red when he realised he'd said that out loud.

'You are most kind,' Circe said, bowing her head. 'And you are?'

'Tim Baker,' he replied, smoothing down his crumpled T-shirt.

'Mmm. I like it. A strong, heroic name. Welcome to my home, Tim Baker.' She entered a large airy room at the back of the house. Circe indicated a table covered with a snowy white cloth. It was laden with overflowing dishes: bowls of fragrant stew, crusty bread, cheese and olive plates, and cakes dripping with honey. 'Take a seat, my dove.'

Tim crossed the room as if he were in a trance. Before he could reach the table, however, something bumped into his legs. He looked down and was astonished to see a large grey pig blocking his path. Tim tried to edge past it. Grunting, the pig moved with him and rammed into his legs again.

Circe nudged the animal firmly aside. She smiled at Tim. 'Here is your vase,' she said, placing it on the floor near the table. 'Do not concern yourself with my pig. I have many animal friends – you may have noticed.'

'I saw them outside. Lions and wolves and bears.'

'Don't be frightened of them. They are gentle. I allow them to come and go as they please. They are the only friends I have,' she said, gazing up from under her eyelashes. 'Not many people come out this way. Now come, eat to your heart's content, and then you may take your leave.'

The pig squealed furiously as Tim pulled out a chair. From the corner of his eye, he noticed Circe give the animal a swift kick. It didn't bother Tim. All that mattered was the food. Mum never let him start with dessert, but he didn't think Circe would mind. Otherwise, why put it all out at once? He selected a cake and bit into it. It was sweet and crumbly and delicious. It was filled with crushed nuts and tasted of cinnamon and cloves.

Tim leant back in his chair and closed his eyes, savouring the taste. The pig continued to squeal ... and then something incredible happened: the grunting, screeching sounds began to make sense.

'I said, do not partake of that meal!' the pig snapped. 'How many times must I repeat my warning?'

Tim's eyes snapped open. 'Odysseus?' he said, but what actually came out was a snort. His hand flew to his mouth ... sort of. It wasn't a hand anymore; it was a trotter! Stunned, Tim toppled out of the chair and found himself snuffling around on the floor.

'Alas, all is lost!' grunted Odysseus. 'As you have joined me in my unfortunate condition, we are without hope.' The powerful warrior looked like a pig and made pig noises, but Tim now understood him perfectly well. He looked down at the pink trotters where his hands should be.

'WHAT HAPPENED TO US?'

Tim wailed, unable to believe what he was seeing.

'Although lovely to behold, Circe is a cunning enchantress. Long ago she lived on a faraway island. My men and I strayed upon her shores. Oh, such dreadful fate!

She enticed my men with a sumptuous feast, which she had laced with a magical potion. When they partook of the food they were transformed into animals. And now it has happened again! I was taking the amphora home when I became entranced by the smell of food. I could not resist.' He grunted unhappily. 'Perhaps I should change my name from Odysseus the Cunning to Odysseus the Idiot.'

'Don't say that,' Tim said. 'She tricked me, too. How did your men turn back into humans last time? Does the magic potion wear off by itself?'

The grey pig swung his head back and forth slowly. 'If only it were so simple. Glorious Hermes came to me in a vision.

"Oh, wretched man," he said, "takest thou of the holy herb moly, which shall protect thee from this enchantress' sorcery.'"

Tim knew that Hermes didn't speak like that. Still, this wasn't the time to split hairs. 'How do we find this holy moly?'

Odysseus was about to answer when there was a knock at the door.

With a contemptuous glance over her shoulder at the two pigs, Circe left the room to answer the door. Tim heard Zoe's voice drifting down the hallway.

'I'm looking for my friend. A weird boy in freakish clothes. Have you seen him?'

Friend! Did that mean Zoe had finally remembered him? Tim tried to jump for joy but tripped over his extra set of legs.

'A boy, you say?' Circe sounded thoughtful. 'No, sweet child, I have not seen him. Perhaps you should come inside and refresh yourself before you resume your search.'

When he heard that, Tim rushed down the hallway, squealing as loudly as he could. Odysseus' trotters clattered on the tiles behind him. Tim ran straight at Zoe and headbutted her knees. He had to stop her from entering! If she ate or drank, their only chance of rescue would be lost.

'WHOA!'

Zoe cried, swinging her arms to regain her balance as her legs buckled.

'Please excuse my companions,' Circe said, putting a restraining hand on Tim's back. 'They are the only friends I have. You may have noticed that I am an animal lover.' She indicated the lions and wolves prowling outside.

Tim thought he understood why the animals were so tame. 'Are they people too?' he asked the warrior. 'Is that why they didn't attack us?'

'I am certain of it,' Odysseus grunted. 'Poor souls. I know not their names nor their circumstance, yet I …' he continued in his lyrical way. Tim tried to block him out so that he could listen to Zoe and Circe instead.

'Your pigs look upset,' Zoe was saying.

'That's because I am talking to you,' Circe said, laughing in a tinkling sort of way. 'They get jealous, the poor dears. But we will not let them distract us! Come inside, have a honey cake and regain your energy. Then we will discuss how to find your friend.'

'If you're sure you don't mind …'

Tim tried to ram Zoe again but was held back by the enchantress. 'Watch it,' she muttered, so that only Tim could hear, 'or I'll turn you into pork chops!'

Tim squealed and ran back to the dining room. He would knock all the food off the table if necessary and trample it underfoot. Anything to stop Zoe from eating. But Zoe didn't enter the room. Instead, she hovered at the doorway.

'Come, my sweet,' Circe coaxed, 'take a seat. Have a cake.'

'Oh, I will,' Zoe said. 'But first let's try this appetiser.' Tim saw the girl draw something out from the folds of her chiton. 'My mother says it refreshes the palate.'

'That is very nice of you,' Circe said. She took the object from Zoe's hands. Tim saw that it was a dark yellow fruit. He held his breath.

'Mmmm,' Circe murmured as she took a bite. 'That is truly delicious. What do you call this fruit?'

'Lotus. Have another.'

'You know, I believe I will! Mmmm. You are such a thoughtful child. People don't normally give *me* anything. At least, I don't think they do.' Circe stopped chewing and looked around. 'What were we talking about?'

'You told me to take that vase and the pink pig and go.'

'Did I, dear?' Circe sounded very vague. 'In that case, take them and go. Leave me some more of that fruit, if you please.'

'Here, take them all.' Zoe grinned, thrusting a handful at the woman. 'Come on, pig, follow me.' Zoe marched down the hallway and out of the front door. Tim and Odysseus kept close behind her and Circe did nothing to stop them.

'Not you,' Zoe said to the big grey pig.

Odysseus let out such an angry squeal that Zoe jumped.

'All right, you too!' she said.

'We must go forth now in search of the holy herb moly,' Odysseus said. 'We are of good fortune, for I have heard tell that it grows wild in these mountains.'

'Great! Did you hear that, Zoe?'

'Do not bother,' Odysseus grunted. 'She cannot understand us, just as you could not understand me before you transformed.'

Zoe looked at Tim. 'We'll go to my house, Tim. Dad will know what to do. Oh, and in case you're wondering – I remember you now. I remember everything. The lotus must have worn off when you got turned into a pig. Actually, you haven't changed that much.'

Tim squealed louder than ever, and Zoe chuckled.

The girl had to carry the vase all by herself. She struggled but walked gamely on. They had only covered a few hundred metres when Odysseus came to a sudden halt. Tim looked around, wondering why the warrior had stopped. Had he hurt himself? It didn't look like it. Rather, he was staring intently at a patch of flowers that looked like tiny white

snowdrops. His snout twitched and his squinty little eyes lit up with delight.

'The miraculous herb! I have found it! Come, let us feast on our salvation.'

Odysseus took off towards the patch and Tim followed.

'Come back,' Zoe called. 'What are you doing? We have to go home.'

Tim didn't bother trying to explain. Instead, he thrust his snout firmly into the patch and started to eat. The flowering herb didn't taste very nice. It was bitter.

Zoe dropped the vase and ran after them. 'Stop making pigs of yourselves,' she cried. 'That's what got you into this mess in the first place!'

Tim kept chewing. The stalks were tough. Grimacing, he swallowed. Was it working? He grunted experimentally.

He still sounded like a pig.

'Eat more,' Odysseus urged with his mouth full. 'It takes more than one bite to transform us.' The big grey pig put his head down and continued munching on the bitter herb.

Tim tore another mouthful of moly, but then he heard something that made him spit it out in shock. It was a yowling, growling sound. Hera's peacocks! How on earth had they found them there? He

snorted out a warning but there was no
need. Zoe was clearly aware of the threat.
She backed away, her head whipping left
and right.

At first Tim couldn't see the birds, but
then they appeared in a golden flash, with
Hera in their midst.

'So,' she hissed, her eyes like daggers.
'At last I have found you.'

Tim pricked up his ears
in surprise. How did she
know who he was? He
still looked like a pig.
Then he realised that
Hera wasn't talking
to him. She was
glaring at Zoe.

'So what?' Zoe shrugged. 'I decided to go for a walk. Not against the law, is it?'

'No, but theft is.' Hera's voice was brittle. 'You took my flask – my property – out of my hands and ran away. I looked everywhere for you and now I find you skulking here. It is an odd place to choose for a walk, wouldn't you say? I believe that you came up here to hide the flask from me.'

Zoe tossed her curls over her shoulder. 'Gosh, now why would I want to do that? The flask isn't important, is it?' Tim had to hand it to the girl. She didn't lack courage.

'The flask, if you please.' Hera held out her hand.

'I don't have it,' Zoe said. She thrust her hands behind her back.

'What did you just put behind your back?' Hera snapped.

'Nothing.'

'Let me see.' Hera strode sideways, trying to get a look. 'Is it the flask?'

'Nope.' Zoe spun around to block the goddess' view.

From Tim's angle, he could see that Zoe's hands were empty. Of course she wasn't hiding the flask: they'd left it at her house with a gaping hole in its side. What was Zoe thinking? Didn't she know that playing games with someone as dangerous as Hera was a bad idea?

'I tire of your childishness. Hand me the flask at once. I know that Timothy Baker is inside it; the foolish boy fell for my trap. You thought to come here and hide him from me? You have failed.'

'I don't have the flask,' Zoe answered truthfully.

'Then I will take that instead!' Hera pointed dramatically at the magic vase, which Zoe had placed on the ground. 'Choose. Give me the flask with your friend inside, or I will take this vase and recapture your father.'

Tim was watching with his mouth hanging open. If Hera took the vase it would be a disaster. She'd trap Hercules – and probably Zoe and Agatha too – out of sheer spite. He had to do something.

'Keep eating,' Odysseus said, tearing at the herbs with his tusks. 'You can only save your friends if you return to human form. There is nothing you can do as a lowly pig.'

'You think so?' Tim grunted. 'Watch me.' With that, he ran straight at Hera.

The goddess squawked involuntarily. 'Help me, my petals,' she called out to her birds. 'A wild animal is attacking me!'

Rather than helping their queen, the peacocks scattered at the sight of the charging pig. At the last second, Tim changed direction. He circled behind Hera and smashed into the back of her knees. With a furious cry, the goddess toppled over.

'Aiee! My hair! My beautiful gown! All covered in dirt! You shall pay for this, filthy pig. I will sacrifice you upon my altar!'

'Not if I have a say in the matter.' Odysseus' voice rang out as clear as a bell. Tim looked up and saw that the powerful warrior had returned to human form. He pulled himself to his full height. Sunlight gleamed off his bronze armour and his tooth-covered cap glistened menacingly. 'Go now, woman, before you anger me.'

'How – how dare you speak to me like that! Do

you know who I am?' Hera struggled to her feet, adjusting her crown which had slipped when she fell. 'I am Queen of Olympus, and you are nobody. A mere mortal. Once your pathetic little life is over, you shall be forgotten – but I will be worshipped for all eternity!'

'Me? Forgotten? I do not think so,' Odysseus said. 'I have heard of a young bard who shall sing my praises to future generations. His name is Homer.' The warrior strode over to the magic vase and picked it up. The muscles on his tanned arms rippled and bulged. 'Now, prise this vase from my grasp – if you can!'

Hera opened her mouth to reply but then paused. 'It matters not,' she said slowly, her lips twisting into a smile. 'Hide the flask if you like. Hold onto that cursed vase. It makes no difference. Timothy Baker is trapped, and will be for all eternity! I will find another way to seek vengeance on the rest of you.' With a triumphant sneer, the goddess disappeared in a cloud of golden sparkles, along with her peacocks.

Grunting, Tim waddled back to the herb patch and took a big mouthful.

'I must take leave of you now,' Odysseus said, after Tim had returned to human form and the explanations were finished. 'I will take an ample supply of the holy herb moly back to Circe's mansion. There I will offer it to the lions, bears and wolves, and allow them to transform back into men. I expect they will need a good tale to enliven their spirits. Fortunately, I will be able to share my experiences–'

'Excuse me,' Zoe butted in. 'I was wondering. What are those big teeth on your head?'

Odysseus' hands flew to his helmet. 'I wore this in the war against the Trojans. Only the mightiest of warriors have them. These are boar's teeth … from wild pigs.' He looked at Tim meaningfully. 'Twelve boars were killed to make this helmet. I could have added another couple of teeth if your young friend here had not eaten the herb fast enough.'

Tim sucked in a breath and Zoe looked aghast.

'That was a joke.' Odysseus' tanned face broke into a grin. 'Some people have no sense of humour.' He walked up to Tim and ruffled his hair. 'But you, young man, have proved yourself worthy. It is a relief to know that the future is in safe hands – even the far distant future.'

It took Tim a moment to realise what he was saying. 'You know I'm a time traveller?'

The warrior nodded. 'My good friend Hercules has often boasted of you.' Tim beamed as Odysseus continued talking. 'Once Hercules begins, it is impossible to turn the subject onto more interesting matters, despite my most fervent attempts. He has an unfortunate tendency to ramble.'

'Hey, that's my dad you're talking about!' Zoe's chin jutted aggressively.

'Indeed? I can see the resemblance.'

Zoe opened her mouth and closed it. She didn't seem to know what to say to that.

'Tell your father that I will visit him directly,' Odysseus continued. 'Once I have restored Circe's victims and regaled them with my tales of struggle, of triumph over adversity, of romance and adventure …'

The warrior was still talking when Tim and Zoe waved goodbye. Tim wore a grin and Zoe a scowl, but together they picked up the vase and headed back to the secret tunnel.

'Why is Hera so keen to trap you?' Zoe asked after they'd walked some distance. 'Athena said Hera's scared of the future and being forgotten, but still. It's not like *you* are a threat to her or anything.'

'Yeah, I've been wondering about that too.' Tim scratched his head with his free hand. 'Maybe she's worried that people in *your* day will start to realise she's not so important. I mean, nobody worships her in *my* day, and we're perfectly fine without her.'

'Huh, maybe. It sounds much better in your time.' Zoe sounded wistful.

'Better in some ways, I guess. Worse in others.'

'Like what?'

Tim shrugged. He was far too tired to answer such a big question. His aching body was begging for rest. Despite that, a warm glow of happiness spread through his chest. Zoe remembered him! The effects of the lotus fruit had worn off and she was his friend again. Chances were that Hercules and Agatha had also remembered him by now. Even if this did have to be Tim's last visit to Ancient Greece, at least he'd be able to say a proper goodbye.

What *was* his time like? 'It's hard to explain,' said Tim, his eyelids beginning to droop. 'We're nearly back at yours.'

As they approached Zoe's home, Tim heard the front door slam. Without a glance at the approaching children, Hera stormed out of the house and strode off in the opposite direction.

'What's she doing here?' Zoe spluttered. 'Did she hurt my parents?'

Alarmed, Tim and Zoe entered the courtyard. They could hear voices coming from one of the rooms. It was Hercules and Agatha.

Zoe let out a gusty sigh of relief. 'Thank goodness they're all right.'

Tim waved at her to be quiet. The adults' voices were grave. What were they talking about?

'We must not let the children know,' Agatha was saying.

It was hard to make out Hercules' reply, but he was clearly upset. Thumping sounds accompanied every syllable. Tim suspected the furniture was getting a beating.

'I don't want them to worry, husband. I am sure that Hera was only bluffing. Tim Baker must return to his mother, and indeed he has probably gone already. If not, keep quiet about this. I do not want him to worry about me.'

Worry about Agatha? What had Hera said to them? Tim raised his eyebrows and Zoe's hand flew to her mouth.

Hercules said something incomprehensible.

'I *am* safe. I have you to protect me.' Agatha replied.

'From what?' Zoe hissed. Tim could only shrug. This didn't sound good.

Zoe couldn't stand it any longer. She stomped into the house. 'What are you two talking about?'

Howling, Hercules threw himself at Tim. He hoisted him in the air and wrapped him in a giant hug. Tears glistened in his eyes. 'Tim Baker, my very good friend! I am sorry that I didn't remember you, but I do now and I will never forget you ever again. Can you find it in your heart to forgive me?'

'Put him down, dear.' Agatha tugged at her husband's chiton.

'Not until he names my penance. Nothing is too much trouble. Order me to count the pebbles on Mount Olympus or to drain the River Styx. Go on, I can do it.'

'There is one thing I want.' Tim wriggled in Hercules' grip.

'Name it and it shall be done.'

'Can you put me down, please?'

'ANYTHING!'

Hercules boomed, and placed Tim on the ground. He dusted him off with a flourish. 'There, is that better?'

'You don't need to do anything! It wasn't your fault,' Tim reassured his friend. 'It was Hera's.'

'What did she say to you? We saw her leaving.' Zoe clenched her fists and looked at her parents. 'Did she threaten you?'

'There's nothing to worry about,' Agatha said in a firm voice. Tim couldn't help noticing that her face was pale.

Zoe stood firm. 'I want to know.'

'It was nothing.'

'Dad?'

'You heard your mother.'

Tim's three friends stared at each other. Not one of them blinked.

Tim smothered a jaw-cracking yawn. If he didn't go to bed soon, he'd fall asleep on the spot. He was worried about his friends, but right now he was far too tired to be of any use to them. Fortunately it didn't look as if there was any immediate danger. Besides, he had the feeling that Agatha wouldn't say anything until he left.

'I think I'd better go now,' he said, swaying with exhaustion. 'I'll come back as soon as I can. I promise.'

'Good idea.'

'You do that.'

'See you then.'

Tim left his friends locked in a three-way stalemate. Even if Mum did decide to sell the vase, he was determined to make one last trip to check that they were okay. He'd get up extra early, before his mother woke up.

The vase deposited Tim gently on his bedroom floor.

'Tim?' His mother's voice drifted up the stairs. 'Dinner's ready.'

He'd rather sleep than eat, but Mum would worry if he skipped dinner. Luckily Tim was alert enough to pull on a long-sleeved shirt. If Mum saw the bruises on his arms she'd ask him what had happened and he was in no state to come up with a plausible explanation. He clumped down the stairs. He should leave all talk of the vase until morning, he decided. He needed to work out exactly what to tell her. Should he explain about his adventures? It was a big decision. He needed to sleep on it.

'Have some lasagne,' Mum said. 'And when we're finished …' She indicated the chessboard on the table. The pieces were all set up, ready to be played.

'Hmm?' He peered at the game through bleary eyes.

'Didn't you say you needed to practise for the chess tournament? Well, you can play against me.'

Tim tried to remember. He and Ajay were in a contest with other schools, and his best friend thought Tim needed to prepare more. 'Yeah, maybe. But I'm too tired today. I can't concentrate.'

'Great!' His mother picked up a queen and beamed at him. 'That means I can't lose.'

Look out for Tim's next ADVENTURE!

HOPELESS HEROES

ODYSSEUS'
TROJAN TRICK

STELLA
TARAKSON

Sweet
Cherry

'Are you sure this is a good idea?' Tim Baker sat with his shoulders hunched. He stared glumly at his best friend Ajay, who was sitting opposite him. 'We've got no chance.' Tim grumbled.

'Don't be like that,' Ajay said. His brown eyes flicked up to Tim's face then back down again. 'We can do it. Now concentrate.' Ajay drummed his fingers on the tabletop and propped his chin on one fist.

Tim could tell that his friend was getting impatient, but he didn't like being pushed. 'Why did we agree to play in the first place?' he moaned. Beads of sweat had broken out on his brow and he wiped

them away with the back of his hand.
'We'll be like lambs to the slaughter.'

'Would you stop being such a
misery guts?' Ajay said, inspecting the
chessboard. 'We've as good a chance as
anyone. Why are you so grumpy?'

'I'm not grumpy,' Tim muttered, even
though he knew he was. There was no
way he could tell Ajay the reason why.

He'd tried sharing his big secret with
his friend back when his adventures first
started, but Ajay hadn't believed him.
Not many people would believe that
the ancient hero, Hercules, had been
trapped in an old Greek vase. Or that he'd
escaped into the modern world when Tim
accidentally broke it. Ajay had thought

it was all a joke. So Tim never told him that he'd also worked out how to travel through time, back to Ancient Greece.

His best friend knew nothing about Tim's adventures with Zoe, Hercules' daughter. Ajay didn't know that Hera, the vengeful queen goddess, hated Tim and was always trying to capture him. This meant Tim couldn't tell Ajay the *real* reason for his grumpiness: he was worried.

Last night, Tim and Zoe had overheard her parents talking. They hadn't been able to catch everything, but they got the gist: Hera had threatened Agatha, Zoe's gentle mother, who had shown Tim nothing but kindness.

And it was all Tim's fault.

'Are you going to make your move or what?' Ajay's eyes flashed with annoyance. 'We haven't got all day, you know.'

Tim heard someone snigger. From the corner of his eye he noticed a figure lurking. He kept his gaze firmly on his chess pieces – he was not in the mood for an audience. Shrugging, he reached out his finger and pushed. 'Bishop to E5,' Tim said, his voice flat.

Ajay's eyebrows flew to the top of his forehead. 'Are you nuts? That leaves your queen wide open. See? I can get her with my rook.' He matched his words with the action.

Tim blinked at the checkered board. 'Oh yeah.'

If only Hera, Queen of Olympus, was that easy to defeat. Tim sighed. Hera feared and mistrusted the future. She wanted to rule forever in a world that never changed, where the Olympians reigned supreme. Yet Tim represented a time when they were all but forgotten. Hera seemed to hate him just for that. And it didn't help that he had defied her several times and won. Now, because Hercules was on Tim's side, Hera was threatening to do something to his wife. Tim didn't know what exactly – Zoe's parents wouldn't tell them – but that only made him worry more. How could he protect Agatha against an unknown threat?

'Are you listening?' Ajay asked tetchily. 'Look at the board. Checkmate in two moves.' He traced the paths his pieces could take with his fingers. 'Maybe you're right,' Ajay added, his lips falling into a frown. 'Maybe we should drop out of the chess club. We'll be a laughing stock.'

Ajay was the school's best player. Tim knew he had been looking forward to next week's match against the posh girls' school. Tim would have been too, if his life wasn't falling apart …

CRASH!

Tim jumped. The sound of the falling chess set was like a thunderclap in the quiet library.

'Hey! Watch it!' Ajay growled, snapping around to face the large boy who loomed over them.

'That's what you get for ignoring me,' Leo snapped, folding his arms across his chest. 'I don't like being ignored.'

Tim looked at Leo warily. Leo had been bullying Tim for years. Tim knew that Leo had problems at home, but that didn't make him any easier to deal with.

'Sorry, I didn't notice y–' Tim started to say, but Ajay interrupted him hotly.

'Can't you see we're busy?' Ajay said to Leo. 'We have to practice.'

'I don't know why you nerds waste your time on this stupid game. Hang on … yeah, I do. You're nerds.' Leo chuckled nastily.

'I'd like to see you do better,' Ajay snapped, scooping up the chess pieces that had fallen on the floor and piling them back onto the table.

'You're on,' Leo said. He pulled up a chair, turned it backwards and straddled it. 'I can beat you at your own stupid game. You first, Cinderella.'

'What?' Tim was surprised that Leo had taken the bait. So surprised that he barely noticed the nickname Leo always taunted him with – a jab at the fact that Tim had to do housework.

'SCARED?'

Leo sneered. 'Know you're going to lose, do ya? Chicken.' He flapped his arms as if they were wings and made loud clucking sounds.

'Shh, you'll get us kicked out of the library.' As he spoke, Ajay swiftly set up the board. 'You can play if you're quiet.'

Tim wondered whether Ajay wanted him to play against Leo so that he'd gain some confidence with an easy victory.

'Bagsy the white pieces.' Leo cracked his knuckles and picked up a white pawn. 'Tell ya what. If I lose, I'll stop calling you Cinderella.' His squinty eyes bored into Tim's. 'But if I win, you've got to do something for me.'

'What sort of something?' Tim asked suspiciously.

Leo shrugged his beefy shoulders. 'Dunno. I'll think of something.'

Tim peered at him through narrowed

eyes. He knew that Leo was on to him. Leo had been at Tim's house, working on a school project. Snooping around, he'd caught Tim on his way to and from one of his adventures in Ancient Greece. Tim had been avoiding Leo ever since, hoping he'd forget about it.

'Come on,' Ajay urged Tim. 'There's no way you can lose against him.'

But Tim did. Leo played cleverly and aggressively and won the match in just a few moves. Ajay, who'd been watching with his mouth hanging open, couldn't wait to challenge Leo himself. Minutes later, Ajay was left scratching his head in amazement as he, too, lost the game in record time.

'How come you're so good at this?' Ajay asked, his hair standing up in wild tufts. 'You should join the chess club! You can partner me in the match next week. We'll win for sure.' Ajay didn't ask whether Tim minded, he noticed.

'Might do,' Leo said carelessly, 'if there's nothing better to do.' Standing up, he cracked his knuckles. 'Don't forget you owe me a favour, Cinderella. See you after school – at your place.'

Tim grabbed his bag as soon as the bell rang. He wanted to get home as quickly as possible, before Leo could catch up with him. To thrash them so easily at chess, the bully couldn't be as dumb as he looked. He knew that Tim was hiding a mysterious secret, but he didn't know what it was.

Tim planned to keep it that way.

Ajay bustled up to him, a worried look on his face. 'You don't mind me asking Leo to partner me in chess, do you?'

'No. It's fine.' It came out more sharply than Tim intended.

'It's just that he's so good,' Ajay said, his eyes widening with worry. 'And you said you didn't want to play anyway …'

'I don't mind, really.' Tim flashed an oversized toothy grin, hoping to reassure his friend. Ajay flinched. 'No, really. It's a relief,' Tim added. 'I'm in a rush, that's all.' He swung his bag over his shoulder and checked that Leo hadn't followed him out of the classroom. He knew he'd be full of questions – questions that Tim did not plan on answering.

'Oh. Hey, what was all that about Leo coming to your place and–' Tim didn't hear the rest of Ajay's sentence. He was already running towards the school gate, without a backwards glance.

■ ■ ■

The magic vase was back on the mantelpiece in the living room. Mum had decided to sell it, and now that she'd found a buyer she'd decided that Tim couldn't keep it in his bedroom anymore. 'If you broke it once, you might break it again,' she had said, matter-of-factly. She still didn't know how Tim had managed to fix it so perfectly. The criss-crossing cracks that had once covered the glued-together surface had mysteriously

vanished, and now it looked as good as new. Of course he couldn't tell her that the messenger god Hermes had fixed it with a simple wave of his hand.

At least Mum hadn't locked the vase away. If she had, Tim would never know whether Agatha was safe.

Tim couldn't tear his eyes away from it. He knew he should be doing the dusting and then his homework. But how could he, when Zoe's mother was in danger? Hera might be after her at this very moment. Or maybe it was too late! Maybe the goddess had already done whatever it was she'd threatened to do.

Tim had to go back and help his friends. He wouldn't have the vase for much longer. Now might be his only chance to fix the problem – once and for all.

Abandoning his chores, he grabbed the vase's black handles. 'Oh vase, take me to Zoe's place,' he said out loud. In his head he added, 'for one last time'.

His feet lifted into the air as the familiar golden mist shimmered around his body. The dizzying flight through time and space used to make him feel queasy, but now he found it unbearably slow. The vase deposited him on Zoe's doorstep and Hercules answered his knock.

'Tim Baker!' the hero boomed, his face crinkling into a delighted smile. 'I didn't think we would see you again. Welcome! Come inside.'

Tim stepped over the threshold into the internal courtyard. By the looks of it, everything was fine. He let out a shaky breath.

'Agatha and Zoe have gone to the well but they promised they wouldn't be long,' Hercules continued. 'Come with me into the andron. A friend of mine is here, and I think you know each other.'

Tim didn't move. He was still trying to calm his nerves. Besides, he'd never been in that room before. 'The andron? B-but … only men are allowed in there,' he stuttered. Women and children – even Agatha and Zoe – couldn't enter the mysterious room.

'That is true.' Hercules stared down at Tim, his face thoughtful. 'But you have changed a great deal since we first met. You have faced many monsters and outsmarted the gods themselves. My friend, I think you have earned your place inside.'

Tim pulled himself up to his full height. The andron! Wow! He'd always wondered what it was like. Zoe would be so jealous if she knew. Holding his breath, Tim followed Hercules inside.

The andron was easily the largest room in the house. A sprawling mosaic covered the floor, its white, grey and black pebbles set in geometric shapes. There were a dozen pictures painted directly onto the plastered walls, each showing Hercules performing one of his

twelve labours. Unlike the other rooms, which showed Agatha's gentle touch, this room was darker and distinctly masculine. Couches that looked like a cross between a bed and a sofa were arranged around the walls. On one of these, nestled among cushions, lounged a familiar figure.

'Tim Baker, youthful friend from the future, I salute you.' The powerful warrior propped himself on his elbow and raised his drinking cup. He was wearing gleaming bronze chest armour. His boar-tooth helmet was tucked beneath his seat. 'Will you be joining us in a toast? I assure you our host provides only the finest of wines.'

'No thanks, Odysseus,' Tim said, trying not to stare at his surroundings. 'I don't drink wine. I'm too young.'

The tanned, middle-aged warrior, who Tim had met on a recent adventure, raised a bristly eyebrow.

'TOO YOUNG?

You disappoint me. Did I say I was too young when I withstood the sirens' song? Did I say I was too young when I hurled a pointed stick into the Cyclops' single eye, thus blinding him and enabling our escape?'

Tim shuddered. That sounded awful. Suddenly he felt even younger. 'I'm only ten.'

'Fie! Did I say I was only ten when I cunningly devised the Trojan Horse and used it to defeat the enemy?'

'Wow, were you only ten then?' Tim asked.

'No … but I fail to see how that matters. Did I say I was only ten when–'

'That will do, Odysseus,' Hercules interrupted, hands on hips. 'Leave the boy alone. Come, let us play a game of astragaloi to pass the time until the women return. Tim Baker may join us if he wishes.'

Not another game! Tim had been expecting grown-up talk, about battles or wars or something equally thrilling. He may as well still be in the library with Ajay.

Tim hoped that this new game was nothing like chess, and was relieved when Hercules pulled out a small cloth satchel. Inside were some knobbly little bones, which Tim recognised as knucklebones. His grandmother had a plastic set that she used to play with as a child. She would throw all the pieces in the air and catch them on the back of her hand. Tim had tried it a few times. It was harder than it looked. Hercules' set was different. There were numbers written on the bones, making them look a bit like dice.

'Do you know how to play?' Hercules asked, squatting on the floor.

'Dad, come quickly!'

Tim jumped when he heard Zoe's voice through the doorway. She sounded upset.

Hercules dropped the knucklebones and sprung to his feet. In one swift motion, he was out of the andron and in the courtyard. 'What's wrong?'

'It's Ma.' Tim caught a glimpse of Zoe's tear-stained face. 'She's gone.'

HOPELESS HEROES

To download Hopeless Heroes

ACTIVITIES
AND
POSTERS

visit:
www.sweetcherrypublishing.com/resources

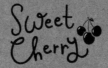

Sweet
Cherry